# DIARY OF A PRIVATE SCHOOL KID

---

## THE INADVERTENT BULLY

## PENN BROOKS

SNOWDROPS

*To St. Francis-St. Hedwig School of Naugatuck:*

*Great memories, wonderful friends, creepy basement.*

# CONTENTS

Dear Archbishop Gregor,

My name is Ben Montgomery and I am a student at one of the schools in your diocese. I would like to raise a very serious issue I have with one of its teachers.

Sister Ellen of St. Guadalupe in Pinewood resorted to cruel and unusual punishment to drive home a point that she was trying to make. I did something wrong, and I can readily admit that. I told her how guilty I felt for doing what I did, and still she gave me this punishment.

This wasn't like detention. That's pretty standard and easy, sitting in a room and twiddling your thumbs. This punishment was far worse - writing lengthy essays about myself in hopes that I get in touch with my feelings. You'll find the evidence of these papers attached to this letter.

I am asking for immediate action in this matter. Maybe providing me with a few bonus days off in trade for the time I spent on these papers. Maybe Sister Ellen has to give me a mandatory A for the classes she teaches. Or what about a free pass to heaven? No? It was worth a shot.

Thank you for your time, your honor.

Forever your sheep,

Ben Montgomery

## DISCLAIMER

Dear Future Me,

Sister Ellen is making me write these essays because she says I need to get in touch with my soul. I am doing this under protest. Please don't think of your past self as some weenie for writing glorified diary entries. For your entertainment (and the benefit of filling up more page space), I am including some pictures.

Sincerely,

Me

## INTRODUCING ME

My name is Benedict Montgomery, but most people call me "Ben" for short. Actually, that's not entirely true. My family calls me "Ben." *Most people* call me "Egg-boy" even though I beg them to stop.

The name evolved from an unfortunate choice in wardrobe one day not too long ago. Like all bad things that happen in school, it turned into this whole big deal that can never be undone.

I should state for the record, that I am <u>not</u> an egg. I am a boy. I'm 10 years old and in the 5th grade at St. Guadalupe's. Every day, I have to wake up and put a tie on to come to school. This stinks because St. Guadalupe's shares the same bus routes as the public schools. I wait at the stop and ride along with the pubbies (that's what we call the public school kids).

Every morning they show off their funny T-shirts, awesome sneakers, and fad accessories. Me? I wear the same dorky thing every day. White shirt. Blue pants.

Penny loafers. And a plaid tie. Plaid: for when it's more important to hide stains than to look good.

At least there is one good thing to come from wearing a tie. It proves I'm a boy. Obviously, eggs don't wear ties.

My class is small compared to the ones they have in public school. There are nine boys including me, and eight girls. That's the entire 5th grade. That number is sure to decrease next year. There has already been talk about a few kids transferring to the public Middle School for 6th grade. I won't have such luck. My parents are completely vested in the belief that private school is the way to go. Phooey! This is my sixth year here and I don't see myself as any better off than those public school kids I ride the bus with. One time I saw a kid go to school in pajamas. How awesome is that? Pajamas! What am I doing here?

My mom tells me I look handsome in the school uniform. She says that a tie is very distinguished. That may be true for a businessman or lawyer, but mine clips together around the back of my neck and constantly loosens. This wouldn't be such a bad thing if we were allowed to unbutton our top button, but we can't. The top button is part of the uniform according to Sister Ellen. So my malfunctioning tie does not make for the most suave look when it droops down on my still-buttoned collar. Oh yes, so distinguished!

I am not the coolest kid in my class, nor am I in the top sixteen. I am dead last. Not only am I dead last in my class, but there are fourth graders that would probably rank higher than me. I'm like the crumbs at the bottom of a potato chip bag. While they should be treated the same as the big ones, they are often tossed away with the bag and discarded.

What I find so ironic and hilarious is that these classmates of mine that think they are so much better than me are huge dorks and dweebs themselves in the eyes of the pubbies. When it comes to the hierarchy of the kids in this town, public always wins. Even the runts of the public school crowd rank higher than the coolest of us cathies (that's their unfortunate nickname for us).

It makes for a very interesting culture on the shared bus system. Take for instance, Josh Baker. He is pretty much the *it* guy in the St. Guadalupe's 5th grade.

I know of at least three girls in my class that would shave her head to go out with him (whatever "going out" means to a 5th-grader). All of the other seven boys in the class fight to have him at their sleepovers, parties and picnics. Josh is pretty much on a seven-weekend rotation with these kids. In this little world of ours, we have our kings and queens. Josh is our grade's king. But as soon as *any* of us step outside of our parochial world, we become losers to the public crowd.

Josh, for instance, tells anyone in our class what to do. If he needs his lunch fetched for him, he has a handful of numbskulls to do his bidding. If he *forgets* his homework, he only needs to say the words "yeah, so last night..." before receiving a copy of the answers. People are always ready and willing to help him because he is what everyone aspires to be or be around.

But let's take Josh out of our isolated 17-student classroom and throw him on a bus ride with pubbies. He becomes less than ordinary. One time this dork from City Side, Stanley, who I would have to imagine is the social waste of his school, had the nerve to come up to Josh and ask him for his seat. Stanley was obviously put up to it. All eyes on the bus watched him walk over to Josh. They watched this trapper-keeper-carrying, light-up-shoe-wearing, Vaseline-haired dork utter a request for the coolest kid in 5th grade to change seats.

I don't think I ever witnessed anything so riveting. Everyone on the bus started muttering to each other about what would happen next. Was Josh going to punch his lights out? Was he going to make Stanley eat his rainbow unicorn T-shirt? Was he going to deliver a verbal drilling that would diminish every ounce of self-worth poor Stanley had? No! None of these. While many assumed that Josh acted based on the intimidating looks he received from the cooler pubbies and not the words of Stanley, Josh still honored Stanley's request.

This forever changed the social hierarchy between our schools.

Josh's one act put every single one of us cathies below all the pubbies. Our plaid ties or plaid skirts became marks of inferiority. Anyone wearing sneakers to school felt entitled to step on anyone wearing brown or black shoes.

The cooler cathies made out okay. Like a pack of wolves, they stuck together. No one wanted to mess with a larger group of kids. The ones that were targeted were those who traveled alone and didn't hang out with the others. So basically, that was me. For the longest time, I flew under the radar. I got on the bus, found a seat and nobody bothered me. But it seems like there is always a need for a doormat, a person to wipe the mud on. Josh's act forged a bond among the public school kids that didn't exist before. The baseball players were cordial to the chess players. The make-up wearers were friendly to the bookworms. If you wore street clothes to school, you were family. If wore a uniform, you were the hostile neighbor.

A sense of family was not present in the cathy group. The same cliques stayed clicking and the outsiders stayed on the outside. Since then, I have become the face of loserdom. No one from St. Guadalupe's ever sits next to me on the bus. Nobody ever helps when a milk carton hits me in the head.

And everyone seems to join in the laughter that involves me licking the school bus floor. I guess I don't blame anyone. As long as I exist, everyone is content in their role. Even Josh seems to be okay with the status quo as long as no pubby dorks mess with him.

So that's me in a nutshell. I am plankton in the ocean that is Pinewood's school system. I guess that makes the other private school kids some kind of bottom feeding fish, and then the public school kids a large carnivore like a shark or narwhal.

Although real narwhals don't bother real plankton that much, so I should rethink this analogy a bit more. The narwhal's in my example bother the plankton A LOT. You get the idea.

## BEST/WORST THING ABOUT SCHOOL

I'm sure you want to hear a glowing answer about why I love coming to school, but I need to be honest and say that there are no redeemable attributes of going to school at St. Guadalupe's. The building is old and smelly. The cafeteria "food" is rank. And the textbooks we learn from contain questionable content.

"Present-day" Europe

By far, the worst part about attending St. Guadalupe's or any private school has to be wearing a uniform. As I said before, it's a symbol that says, "Hello world! I'm second-rate!" It's much like wearing a sign on your back that reads, "Kick me."

Aside from the negative social side effects that come from wearing a uniform, another downfall is the need for a highly efficient laundry system at home. There are five days of school per week. So I have five shirts, five pants and five pairs of socks that fit me. The key here is the part about them fitting me. About half of my entire wardrobe is made up of school-related stuff. I have some shirts from last year that fit, but are a little too snug. I have pants that are the same way.

Now in a perfect week, I should wear a new pairing each day I go to school. Since we do just about everything in our uniforms (recess, gym, art, etc), we get it fairly dirty. At the end of these days, I put my uniform in my hamper at home. Then on Saturday or Sunday, my mom does the laundry and PRESTO! A new week begins with a clean slate of clothes.

That is the ideal plan. Unfortunately, that is not the reality. I come home each day and throw my dirty clothes in the hamper. That part of the story is consistent so far. However, the amount of times my mom actually does my laundry when she is supposed to is like one in four. So what happens on the following Monday? I have to tap into the year-old backups that don't fit any more. These are tough days, both physically and mentally. I have to endure the pain of being squeezed in the waist and thighs and choked in the neck. And remember, I can't unbutton my top button.

The mental torture comes from dealing with the comments all day long. How many comebacks can one person make to "where's the flood?"

Now we are done with day 8. I have used up my five days of clean, properly-fitting clothes _and_ my clean, snugger-fitting clothes. All but two times, my mom pulled through and did an emergency weekday wash. But those two times she didn't, things got really bad.

The first time it happened, I got through the 8-day cycle. On the ninth day, I had to reuse an old uniform. You might not think that is a big deal since there are many people who wear things more than once before washing. That wouldn't be a problem if I prepared for it. My problem was that I put the clothes in my disgusting, locker-room-scented, toe-cheese filled hamper.

Day 9 is really really bad.

The first time I had a Day 9, I managed to get out of the house without being analyzed by either parent (morning time can be hectic). I first noticed how bad the odor was when I boarded the bus.

Kids scooted as far toward the window in order to avoid contact with me as I walked down the aisle. I decided to test the magnitude of the odor's power by going straight to the back. You know that little seat by the rear door? I never got to sit there before. Usually the hot shot of every bus gets that seat. Well Theo kindly gave it up to me on that day. I was invincible!

As the day went on, the smell got a lot riper. Our school doesn't have any cooling system, so the air can get pretty stagnant. When we all returned from recess, the heat we all gave off made the odor linger. It took on a life of its own. Jordan, who sits in front of me, passed out at one point. Literally. He turned around to look at the clock on the wall and then conked right out.

I don't think Sister Ellen could come out and say it, but I sense she was giving me a lesson on the ABC's of hygiene when she discreetly handed me a pamphlet about personal cleanliness.

Surprisingly, the insults were disappointing. I felt it was a wasted opportunity for some funny comments. Unfortunately, the cleverest remark was the easiest. Since the smell was reminiscent of eggs, I became *Eggs BENedict,* or *Egg-boy* for short. Once that came out of the bag, everyone latched on and didn't let it go.

When I came home, the smell had gotten so bad that my mom finally took notice. When she greeted me at the front door, one small whiff was all she needed to keep me out. I had to disrobe on the screen porch before I was granted access to the house. My mom asked me how I could let myself leave the house like that. I countered with the argument that she should not have let my laundry get out of control. In hindsight, that was a bad thing to say.

The second time a Day 9 came around, my mom was nowhere to be found. She, my Aunt Cheryl and some of their friends went on ladies-only vacation. She left my dad alone to take care of my sister and me. There must have been a miscommunication before my mom left, because none of us had clean laundry. This is not a big deal to my dad or sister, because they aren't bound by having a daily uniform, for me it was déjà vu for disaster. While I probably should have pointed out the lack of clean clothes the night before, I failed. I woke up and went to extract the outfit from the hamper and I couldn't bring myself to do it. The memory of my last Day 9 (or at least the memory of the smell from that day) plagued my mind. I did the noble thing. I told my father about the lack of clean clothes. At first, he thought I was exaggerating. Then I proved it to him and made him a believer.

We tried to do an emergency load of wash. The "quick wash" feature only takes 20 minutes, so we chose that, but my dad didn't realize that the hot water was on. The clothes came out clean, but my white school shirt turned light blue – a major violation to the school uniform code. It was unwearable.

Not only did I effectively reduce my wardrobe cycle by one day, I also had to go back into the hamper and get another uniform set. On top of smelling gross and looking wrinkled, I was now going to be late for school. My dad had to drive me there.

Before he dropped me off, he thought it would help if I slipped his car freshener in my pocket. You know those little Christmas tree things people hang in their car? His was brand new and very strong. I quickly found out that it did <u>nothing</u> to mask the smell. It only enhanced it.

After that day, my parents (headed by my dad's fear of ever smelling that smell again) ensured the laundry cycle would never get that far again. So far, it hasn't, but I don't think I will ever feel secure.

## DESCRIBE YOUR HOME LIFE

Things at home are a lot different than they are at school. I find myself not being tortured or ridiculed on a consistent basis. That is not to imply that I am praised or coddled, though. I fit in somewhere in between, like a backdrop to the chaos.

I have a dad, a mom, and a four-year-old sister, Samantha. They all call me "Ben". Actually, there are many times my parents call me "Benjamin Matthew," but those times usually coincide with me getting in trouble.

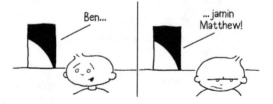

Sometimes, this is handy. It gives me the heads up on whether to answer them or not.

Life at home is not as stressful as it is at school, but it's not without the drama. I tend to have a different outlook on life than my parents and this certainly leads to some conflicts.

For instance, I like TV. A lot. It is my lifeblood. I am pretty sure the gentle glow of the television screen is a bundle of heaven's rays stuffed into a plastic-and-glass box.

I contend that it not only provides a source of entertainment during life's most boring moments, it is also somewhat educational. My parents told me that I have to actually watch educational programming for me to make that argument.

I contend that *The Real Wizards of Beverly Hills* teaches valuable lessons in social interaction.

I find it very hypocritical that my parents have taken such a negative stance toward television. Whenever the first of the month comes around, they do nothing but encourage the watching of it.

During the week, most of my free time is ruined by homework. Since I don't have any reliable friends, I have to do it all by myself. Most of the other kids use their bus buddy to divvy up the workload. It's a smart tactic, but one that I can't use (since I lack said buddy).

When there is a light amount of homework, I can typically fly through it in a half hour. My mom or dad check it and then I can go on my merry way. On nights where I have a heavier load, especially with harder material, I am parked at the kitchen table until supper.

I try to enlist the help of my parents and trick them into giving me the answers.

But they picked up on that long ago. I feel like I'm a smart kid, but my homework certainly doesn't reflect that. After 6 hours of school, my mind needs to rest and charge its battery. Homework prevents this from happening. I get home and all I want to do is relax. My little sister will bounce all over me and want to play. I'd almost consider playing dollies if it got me out of homework, but it's no use. Within minutes of coming home, I have my papers out and ready to start.

My dad owns a business where he divides a lot of his time between the office and home. When he is working from the house, he sets up at the kitchen table and works right alongside me while I'm doing my stuff. I'm not quite sure what he does exactly, but usually it's very intense.

My mom is a part-time nurse and works three nights a week. Those are usually the same days my dad works from home. It's kind of funny that it's either one or the other who is home during the week. Actually, now that I think about it, I rarely see them together. I'm sensing some type of secret identity happening here.

Those times when the family does manage to get

completely together, it's always somewhat awkward. My mom insists we sit down and have a family meal (that nobody else wants to have) and talk about each other's lives. What makes it so uncomfortable is that she goes to these index cards filled with conversation topics. She's not limited to using them at home either. She will pull them out at a restaurant too.

My dad always ends up either talking or texting on his cell phone about halfway through dinner because of business. Mom will go crazy on him that he is not *engaged* in the conversation.

Then he will go on talking about how these calls and emails are what enable them to have meals like the ones we are currently eating. Then my mom will say that she works too, and pretty "darn" hard. So they end up fighting and Sam and I giggle at each other across the table because we know we don't have to answer any more stupid questions.

Over the summer, my mom strives to do more than just have a dinner to bring the family together. She spends months in advance planning a vacation for the four of us. This always results in a huge backlash from the rest of us, because our ideas of vacation vastly differ.

The word vacation sends images of huge roller coasters and water slides racing through my head. I can't contain the excitement of a road trip to Florida.

But as my mom's planning unfolds, she starts sensing the need for more "education" to make the trip worthwhile. So our road trips typically bring us back in time.

So that is how butter is made.

On a more regular basis, it's difficult for the family to agree on a group activity. On the weekends for instance, everyone scrambles to fit in all of the activities that they wanted to do themselves. For my dad, that is work on house projects.

My mom tries to find a quiet place to read her books that we're not allowed to touch or sometimes even look at.

My sister's routine is not all too different. She runs around like a maniac no matter who is home and no matter what day it is. Her behavior is slightly more magnified on the weekend, because no one else is paying any attention to her. The house becomes as wild as the jungle.

She is not the average four year old. She is regularly starved for attention and struts about the house banging pots and pans so we notice.

However, my parents instruct me not to give her the attention she seeks. The theory is that ignoring undesired behavior will encourage the person to stop doing it. Does that work? Nope. She just bangs louder.

So while my parents try to escape somewhere and hide, I am usually left keeping "an eye" on my sister. But if I decide to build things with my Legos, she finds a way to break them apart. If I decide to doodle on some paper, she nudges my arm so I mess up. If there is a video game I want to play, she usually interrupts with random button slapping or remote control nabbing.

My pleas for someone to intervene are usually not heard.

Which means that I am the only person in the family who never gets to do what I want to do. This has become my life, week in and week out.

## WHEN HAVE YOUR ACTIONS LED
## YOU ASTRAY?

I once had the brilliant idea for getting out of the house on a Saturday and have the day all to myself. For weeks, I hinted at a BIG science project that was coming up, and I had to do some research for it. I suggested to my parents that on one of the upcoming Saturdays they drop me off at the public library to work on it.

(How my mind remembered the downtown area.)

The library happened to be down the street from a huge electronics store. My plan was to ditch the library when the coast was clear and mosey on down to Good Buys to play their demo video games in peace.

That Saturday finally came and my dad volunteered to bring me. He dropped me off out front. He told me that he had errands to run and would be back in two hours. Perfect! I filled my backpack with a bunch of books just to make sure I looked good and ready to study. I probably went overboard, because even the short walk into building made my back ache. I waited five minutes for good measure (my dad likes to check his cell phone for emails and messages whenever he has the opportunity). I peaked my head outside and he was gone. Time to go play!

I got about a hundred feet from the exit when I realized a small monkey wrench in this plan. There was no way I would be able to enjoy myself for two hours with the huge bag on my back. Plus, Good Buys doesn't have any chairs set up at their store for video game play. I didn't want to be standing around with this thing on for that whole time. I had to go back.

I set my stuff up on an empty table and made sure it looked like I could come back at any second. I even started writing a paragraph on a blank page in my notebook and left the pen on that page. This was a nice touch. Thirty minutes had gone by, but there was still plenty of time to play.

I didn't anticipate the distance to be quite so far. Usually when we drive downtown, the distance between the library and Good Buys whizzes by. I thought it couldn't be more than two blocks. Maybe it was the humidity taking its toll. Perhaps it was the fact I miscalculated and the distance was more like five blocks. Whatever the case, it took like fifteen minutes to get there.

When I entered the store, I wasted no time and made a B-line to the video section.When I got to the game section, I found the coolest demo possible and grabbed the controller. No one would be taking it from me for the next fifty-eight minutes.

I played for a solid three before I heard the worst possible set of words you could hear in my situation.

My dad was there! Good Buys was on his errand list? Maybe he was shopping for me? Nope! There wasn't a holiday or birthday in the foreseeable future. This trickster of a father of mine was using my study time for his personal gain. How dare he!

I freaked out. I couldn't make it down to the other end of the aisle before they rounded the corner. The only thing I could do was dive behind some video game chairs set up across from the demo.

There I sat as my dad and the salesperson walked down the aisle. My dad seemed to take some particular interest in the video game that I had just been playing.

Maybe *interest* is too weak of a word, because my dad became engrossed with the demo.

I spent the next forty-five minutes crouched behind the boxes across the aisle, waiting for my dad to get bored and to move along. He never moved. Actually, it was pretty impressive how well he did on the game. In that time, he beat three levels and unlocked a few hidden treasures that I never even heard of. I'm starting to wonder if the reason why he's always telling me to get off the video games is so he can play himself.

The salesman urged him a few times to see other set-ups and even try other games, but my dad had none of it. He was like a man possessed on that controller. The whole time, my back was growing sorer from crouching under the shelf and my butt was starting to go numb.

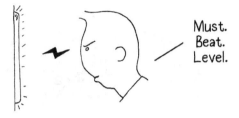

Finally, as it came closer to the time he had to leave to pick me up, he graciously thanked the salesman for his time.

When they walked away, I burst out from behind the boxes ready to sprint. I needed to beat my dad outside, but the first stride I took sent me collapsing to the ground.

Both legs were fully asleep!

I shook them like crazy to get the blood flowing back into them. A man walked by with a frightened look on his face, shielding his young son from the sight of me.

By the time I got my feet to stop tingling, it was too late. I ran to the front of the store just in time to see my dad get into his car. At that point, I should have cut my losses and admitted to the charade. At least this way, I would have had a ride back.

But that's not how it happened. At that moment, I was

sure I could sprint back to the library faster than he could drive there. Three traffic lights stood in between Good Buys and the library. I was counting on a little help from the big Guy upstairs to make those lights red for as long as possible. And so, without any more hesitation, I darted off down the street.

But then it began pouring...

Do you know how hard it is to run in the rain? First, your clothes get wet, which is uncomfortable in itself. Then as they become soaked, they get incredibly heavy! It's like five extra pounds thrown onto you. When it starts flowing into your shoes, you have another problem entirely. The water that soaks into the inner padding turns each step into a suction cup against the bottom of your sole.

So sprinting the five blocks back to the library was hard enough before, now I have to do it wet and weighed down.

I got a really good head start on my dad. He just got into his car when I started my run. With his usual sequence of checking messages and adjusting mirrors three times over, I figured I would have been three quarters of the way by the time he pulled out of the parking lot. I was wrong. With about two and half blocks left to go, I looked out to the road and saw him driving by. I had to duck behind a mailbox to remain unseen.

Avoiding my dad wasn't my only problem. As I came closer to the library, I noticed something in the hands of someone leaving the building – my backpack (my really

really nice backpack)! I recognized the face. It was some dirtbag 5th-grader from City Side who rode our bus to a friend's house on one occasion. He ran out to a car parked in front, using my backpack as an umbrella.

"Hey!" I shouted, but the kid didn't grant me the courtesy of a response. He got into the car and it drove away pretty quickly after that.

There was no use in chasing the car. It cleared a city

block in a matter of seconds. There was another issue I had to contend with. My dad's car was parked right outside the library and he wasn't in it.

I hurried inside and found the study table that I had set up. But before I could situate myself to start "studying" again, my dad showed up.

There were a couple of details that I didn't consider. Firstly, I was literally dripping water like a faucet. A big sloshy puddle pooled beneath me.

Secondly, I was panting and still trying to catch my breath from the run over here.

Even though I avoided eye contact with my dad, I could sense his furrowed eyebrows clench tighter and tighter as he glanced over the scene.

Surprisingly the first words out of his mouth weren't too bad.

When I finished stacking my books, my dad lifted up the pile and took it to the car. Surprisingly, he doled out no punishment. He just demanded that I go dry off.

I went to the only place in the library I could accomplish that.

Surprisingly, the hand dryer worked pretty well. The location, however, wasn't the best place to be stripping down.

When I finally dried off, I left the building and got into my dad's car. I thought he was going to lay into me at that point and lecture me on the importance of trust and responsibility. I was wrong. He simply put the car in gear and drove off.

The entire ride home, my nerves grew shakier and shakier. The longer he drove without speaking; I knew the punishment would be that much harsher. The scowl on his face never relaxed. It was like he was having a hard time deciding on what to do with me.

The stormy weather added to the tension. It was my own mental horror movie. What is he going to do with me? The more he could think about it, the harsher he would be.

I couldn't take it anymore...

My dad's reaction to this confession was slightly unexpected.

My dad pulled the car over immediately so we could talk. It turned out that he was completely oblivious to everything that happened to me. He never realized that I was out of breath or my bag was missing. And while I was soaking wet, he said he figured I got caught in the rain while stretching my legs.

His overly dramatic reaction to my confession was due to his surprise that I was at Good Buys and saw him playing video games for nearly an hour. Apparently, he was supposed to be out running errands that he was able to finish at the local hardware store in a matter of minutes.

We struck a deal with each other, agreeing to keep it secret between us. It turned out that dad was just as afraid of getting in trouble as me. Our agreement tied up every loose end, except for the missing backpack.

Part of our agreement was that I would try to retrieve it back from the pubby who took it. In the meantime, he would cover me as I took an old one out of retirement.

## WHAT ITEM EMPOWERS YOU?

What is this supposed to mean? Like an iron suit that can fly and shoot lasers? Or a hammer that destroys everything around me? Because if that's what you're getting at, I have nothing of the sorts.

I don't have any weapons of any kind, actually. My requests to have a BB gun were swiftly shot down (no pun intended). Same goes for a bow and arrow. I once made a slingshot out of sticks and a thick rubber band. That was confiscated as soon as I nicked the paint job on my mom's car.

I had a baseball bat, but I had to donate it when I stopped playing the sport. The old broomstick in the garage can be used as a ninja bo, but I think it might snap in 14 different pieces if I connected with any target. Do water guns count as weapons?

Back away, perp!

Maybe if I took some coffee cans, some old toothbrushes, and a deck of playing cards, I could...

## WHAT ITEM EMPOWERS YOUR MIND?

Okay, Sister Ellen. You stopped me in the middle of my awesome idea to explain what you meant by something empowering me. It sounds like you want me to talk about something that empowers my mind or emotions - not something that actually gives me an edge in battle. You can see the confusion. Your explanation would have been useful *before* I started writing.

Let me think. Can a fear empower you? The thing that usually keeps me out of trouble is the fear of being in parochial school forever. I have seen glimpses of older kids in college. They always seem very happy.

My cousin is in his second year at school and he talks of three hour school days, wearing sweatpants all of the time, sleeping until noon on a regular basis, eating as much as you want, and playing video games for as long as your thumbs can handle it.

This is the life that I strive for. I don't want to be in this school forever. While I despise homework, the thought of a better life keeps me trudging through it.

Outside of learning and school, my life has been made better by a little book that Santa put in my stocking one year. "Sarcastic Replies and Insults" was something I saw advertised on TV in between cartoons. The commercial for it was hilarious.

You see what they did there? "S'cool" is short for "so cool." And it sounds a lot like "school." It was s'clever.

The commercial also claimed over a hundred new insults to help you get back at bullies.

Hilarious! I didn't really get this one at first, so I asked my mom. She told me that the government officials like to raise taxes and take money for themselves. So comparing the bully to one was political satire. I could just see the praise coming my way.

Once I saw the ad, I knew I must have the book. It promised to improve wit and sarcasm by not using bad or mean words. In a sneaky way, you can insult someone without them really even noticing. I guess part of that is true anyway.

When I discovered the book on Christmas morning, all of the toys and video games quickly drifted into the background. I immediately put it to use.

There were put-downs for the old:

Hey dad, you are *so* gray... cloudy skies get depressed looking at *you.*

Jokes for the young:

Sam, you are *so* young... your birthdays are counted with negative numbers.

Insults for friends:

Comebacks to be used on parents:

I wasn't as good with comebacks toward more threatening adversaries, though:

I would need to do some more studying. I started taking notes, writing things down in a composition notebook. This was a trick that my college cousin taught me. It's supposed to help with reading retention.

From the days going forward I began understanding what older kids were talking about when they talked their talk. When they called Chrissy (whose parents are vegetarian) a leaf-eater, I got what that meant and why they said it. When they were comparing Mrs. Dorian's dogma class with having a colonoscopy, I knew that meant it was a *pain in the butt*.

I soon realized that some of the stuff written in this book didn't quite uphold the promise of the advertiser.

It turned out the book was filled with questionable content. There were words that I never even heard that just sounded wrong rolling off my tongue.

The next day, there was a huge story on the evening news that blew the lid off that book.

Mom confiscated the book within seconds of that airing.

She may have taken my book, but she couldn't take my memories (or my notes that she knew nothing about). I reviewed those notes relentlessly for future reference. I wanted to be able to retrieve them from the back of my brain when I most needed them.

So while I may not have been a boy scout filled with the

knowledge from a field guide to nature, I was definitely empowered with knowledge that I need in the jungle that is my life.

## DISCUSS THE INCIDENT ON THE BUS

So it has come to this? I knew all of this free writing stuff was just a way to get me talking about what happened that day on the bus. Like I told you before, I didn't do anything wrong. However, if you insist on making me tell you EVERY detail, here we go.

It's funny how so many things in life connect at one moment. Last Monday was an example of this.

That morning, I boarded the bus as usual. I found my typical empty seat somewhere between the members of both schools. I thought it would be just another average Monday until the bus turned down a road it never turned down before.

The bus stopped and opened its doors. A new student? In the middle of the year no less? Even though a flash of excitement shot through me, it quickly faded once that student boarded.

I couldn't believe my eyes. The bus picked up the dirtbag pubby who stole my backpack! I told you earlier that I had seen him once before. He rode home one Friday with two pubbies named Dirk and Nelson. He was only visiting them at that time. Besides him running by me in the rain, I hadn't seen him since. Now he was boarding *our* bus. Unfortunately, Dirk and Nelson were seated right in front of me. So naturally, this cretin found the empty spot next to me.

While he was making nice with the goons in front of me, I couldn't help but notice something familiar.

I looked it up and down to make sure I had the right one. Same olive green fabric. Same black leather straps. He sat there rubbing his prized acquisition right in front of my face!

He must have caught me looking at his – no wait – MY bag, because he turned to me and gave me a polite nod of the head.

What a jerk! He was rubbing the whole pubbies-are-better-than-cathies thing right into my face. So you know what I said?

That'll teach him.

The bus stopped at City Side first, before heading over to St. Guadalupe's. Between the times we introduced each other and him being dropped off, I analyzed the situation. This Sante character didn't know that he was wearing my backpack. Advantage: Ben. If I could figure out some way to get it off his back, then I could sweep in unexpectedly and reclaim it!

He got off the bus, not expecting my plan for revenge.

I was utterly useless in class that day. I was so driven by the thought of avenging the theft of my bag, I couldn't concentrate on anything else. I think there might have been a test that day.

Unlike most people, I had only myself to count on. I had no allies in this plot. The act would likely be one (me) against three (Sante + Dirk and Nelson).

Was I prepared to have my head beat in by these three? No. But I started analyzing the probability of that happening.

I don't go to their school. There is never a time where I would run into these three guys outside of the bus – and the bus driver is always ready to stop any horseplay. So I figured I was in a better position to confront them than a bottom-feeder from their own school.

If a person like Stanley tried anything, he would surely get beat up in a bathroom or locker room.

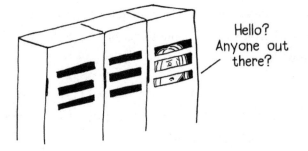

I could take some chances since I probably will never run into these guys outside of the bus. Getting the backpack off Sante would be the difficult part. What kind of distraction would it take? I considered spilling water on him but I didn't want to ruin my backpack.

If we happened to have the same seats as the morning ride, I could use the heater underneath the bench to raise the temperature of the bus. There is a little knob on the outside that controls the heat. Making it hot and uncomfortable might make him take my backpack off. Then when it's time for me to get off, I can dart out the door with it.

This wasn't a bad plan, but it depended on Sante sitting in that same seat and leaving an empty place for me. I can't count on that happening.

There was the possibility of just flat-out telling on him, but I might suffer a greater backlash.

My reputation is bad enough. I don't need to be labeled as the school rat on top of it.

After all these considerations, I came up with the simplest approach – confrontation.

After thinking about it longer, I came to realize that Sante was being nice to me because he didn't yet understand the social hierarchy on our bus. He treated me as an equal. I could use that to my advantage and take him by surprise. If Sante were in an uncomfortable position, he may willingly hand the bag over.

Dismissal that day could not come soon enough. The buses pulled up to our school, having already picked up the kids from City Side. I hopped on board and found Sante seated alone - just as I hoped.

With a deep breath for courage, I approached him.

He politely moved over. So far so good. I opted to stay standing, you know, to seem more intimidating. Then I went right to my point.

The next few moments are somewhat of a blur. I am pretty sure that I transformed into someone else. My brain summoned weeks' worth of studying insults and comebacks and started spewing them out of my mouth.

I was amazed; I actually delivered an appropriate response. I wasn't the only one surprised. A crowd quickly formed around me. Both pubbies and cathies looked on with stunned faces as the lowly "egg-boy" picked a fight with one of the cool kids.

The crowd *ooooooed*. Nobody really had any idea what would happen next. Those kids, Dirk and Nelson, tried to get his back, but I held them off just fine too.

Those two clammed up quick. A few of the cathies snickered and pointed as the two pubbies turned backed around. Sante had a moment on the offensive, but luckily I had an equally effective response.

I got laughs. A lot of laughs.

One might say too many laughs.

Sante got really mad. He turned bright red and looked like he was on the brink of punching me. At that point, I shouldn't have added fuel to the fire.

The other kids loved it. I loved that they loved it. I never felt that level of admiration toward me before. It was comforting. The problem with not getting positive attention too often is that when it happens, you feed off it like it's candy. At that moment, I had a truckload of chocolate sitting before me.

With students from both schools cheering me on, the time had come to end the fight and get my pack back. I went in for the kill.

Now, I know I was out of line from the moment I started this engagement with Sante. I said some fairly crumby things, but this one stung the most. You see, the problem was that it hit a little closer to his chest than anything else since he, as I later found out... was really abandoned by his birth mother (It probably wasn't because he was ugly, but just regular reasons).

So with a dagger to the heart, something happened that I didn't expect – he cried. And it wasn't a gentle whimper. He balled. Tears streamed down his face and he started hyperventilating. Then, when he looked up and saw the eyes of twenty bus riders staring back at him, he couldn't take the embarrassment. He pushed me out of the way and ran off the bus.

The bus didn't roll out until about ten minutes later because the driver and several other teachers went looking for Sante. They could not find him within that timeframe and the driver had to leave without him. For the kids on board, their days were set back a few minutes. Some got home later than expected, and I'm sure the school got some angry phone calls from parents. That's why many of those kids call it the "bus incident."

For me, who had to get off the bus before it was permitted to leave, I think "fiasco" would be a better word to describe this *incident*. After the school called my parents, I had to help find Sante, who could have been anywhere. The whole time that me, some teachers and some school aides searched, Sister Ellen lectured me on why it isn't divine to call people names and make them feel lesser than they are. I argued the fact that it isn't divine to steal other people's belongings either. She quoted some Bible passage about why it isn't good to seek revenge. I stopped listening.

Eventually, we did find Sante.

Sister Ellen made us shake hands and swear that what happened will never happen again.

Some interesting facts came up during our open and moderated conversation. Firstly, it turned out that Sante did not steal my backpack after all. He even proved it.

I was grasping for straws. I knew it was his, but I just didn't want to believe it. I had been wrong the whole time. And I must have been pretty dumb and oblivious to lose the bag in the first place. These notions were not sitting well with me.

Teachers made me apologize, but to be honest, I would have anyway. I genuinely felt guilty about the whole ordeal with Sante. I treated him in a way that I never would want to be treated. I explained this realization to Sister Ellen, and she said that she wouldn't punish me. Instead of having a week's worth of detention, however, I got something far worse.

I see some extra writing assignments in your future.

I pointed out that her assignments were, in fact, punishments because they are in response to an action that she deemed undesirable.

She said that an opportunity to explore oneself and to improve should not be viewed as a punishment. I still disagree with her.

At home, my parents were not as willing to take the reform approach.

They kept asking me if I knew how much my school costs them. I did not. They never told me. Apparently knowing how much it cost would make me not do bad things? I didn't understand their angle.

When the dust (and my parents) settled, we all realized there was one big thing missing in this whole story. My backpack.

My mom went on a tear, which included yelling at my dad for covering me. She told him that I wouldn't have been in such trouble if he did the right thing and helped find the backpack in the first place.

My dad made a call to the library and sure enough...

Once I heard where they found it, everything made sense. I emptied my bag and hung it off the chair.

Once I saw Sante with the same exact bag, I was so caught up by the thought he stole it, I just assumed it was gone. I never bothered to turn around.

## LESSONS LEARNED

I learned that jumping to conclusions can get you in trouble. I learned that treating people poorly makes you feel bad too (and can result in consequences like writing ridiculously long essays).

There was one other thing that developed from this whole fiasco. Something unexpected happened the next day that made me realize an important concept.

I learned that by standing up for myself (even though I was wrong), I got some newfound respect. And instead of people calling me "Egg-boy" or ignoring me altogether, they were actually calling out for me. And using my actual name!

And I'm starting to enjoy that...

*No, No, No! Benjamin, gaining respect through bullying is not a lesson learned! I think there may be more writing assignments in your future...*
*— Sister E*

# More from Penn Brooks

"Fun times. Funny ties."

I hope you enjoy Diary of a Private School Kid. If you'd like to keep reading more of Ben Montgomery's misadventures, check out *Hot Dog Day*, the sequel to the book you're reading now.

Despite a solid attempt to justify his actions, Ben's quest for food lands him in hot water at school - much like the very hot dogs he's trying to obtain. Through a series of head-knockingly bad choices, Ben learns that deception, lies and trickery are not always ways to get what you want.

Get a **free sneak preview** by going to the link below:

## www.pennbrooks.com/book2

## ABOUT THE AUTHOR

Penn Brooks is a former cathy with 12 years of parochial experience under his belt. He currently lives in New England, where he writes, draws and avoids wearing plaid ties.

pennbrooks.com

me@pennbrooks.com

 facebook.com/pennbrooks

CPSIA information can be obtained
at www.ICGtesting.com
Printed in the USA
LVHW031720240919
632125LV00012B/1607/P

9 781726 713474